Once upon a time, there was a young and happy turtle, living with his friends in a small river that was flowing inside a Jungle.

He had a really good and happy life
with many friends.

He was always with his friends, in the river or in the Jungle playing.

He was really enjoying his live along the river.

In the river, he had many freinds like ducks.

He was sometimes talking with the frogs and the little bears.

Hens and ducks liked him too much,
they were singing for him

He was also dear to the elephant
and the Fox.

The rabbits were telling jokes to him and he was always laughinn to the sweet jokes of the rabbits.

Even the Lion the king of the Jungle
was   also   his   friend.

One day he made a decision. He wanted to make one of his dreams finally true. He wanted to swim in a big   sea.

He talked about his decision with his friends, that he is going to swim in a big sea.
His friends told him, that it is a dangerous decision. Big seas are polluted with plastic and garbage.

His friends told him, that plastic and garbages in the seas will make him sick. But he didn't hear his friends advice and started to swim in the big sea direction.

On the way to the big sea, ducks saw him and asked, „where are you going my friend?"
He told, „to the big Sea." They told him that the big sea is polluted, and he must not go there.
But he didn't want to hear them.

On the way to the big sea, he saw the turtles from the next village. They also told him not to do this.

When the Zibras knew that, they also wanted to stop the turtle, but they also couldn't do that.

The sheeps also told him not to go there.

The little girl that was living beside
the river saw and told not to do that.
Because, big seas are polluted now,
too much plastic and micro plastic
are in the seas.

Finally he reached th sea, he didn't find the sea as he was imagining. The sea was dirty with many plastic bags and garbages floating in the sea.

He dreamed of a clean an beautiful sea, but now the sea was full of garbage and Plastic

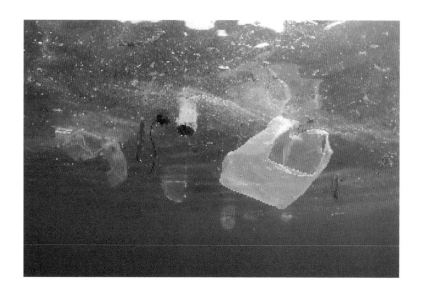

The young turtle was disappointed and after a long way really tired and hungry. Far away he noticed a jelly fish. He swimmed towards that and queckly ate it. But it was not a jelly fish.

After eating the Plastic bag, the turtle became very sick, but he was fortunate, because, a good person found him on the beach and took him to the docotor.
The doctor took out the plastic bag from his stomach and he was cured.

He joined once again his friends and promised to always lesson to his friends and to their advices.

He started a peaceful life with his friends and was always enjoying the life in the clean river and wished that this river always remain clean and natural, forever.

End

The plastics that we are using, remain in the nature for a long time. It takes a lot of years for the plastic to be degraded in the nature. The wind carries the plastic in the seas and Oceans.

The turtles mistakenly eat plastic bags for jelly fish. Because, plastic bags in the oceans look like jelly fish. In order to keep the seas and oceans clean, we must not throw the garbages and plastic everywher.

We have to even clean our nature by collecting the plastic and garbages to have nice and blue rivers and more golden fish and turtles.

Do you like this book or don't like this book, or you have suggestions to improve this book, please write us an email:

Lerner.Book@gmail.com

Please write your openion about this book as a review on Amazon. For every review on Amazon, we will donate 2 USD for street kids of Afghanistan.

Printed in Great Britain
by Amazon